The Princess and the Pizza

by **MARY JANE** and **HERM AUCH**

Holiday House / New York

In memory of Eunice Kolligian,
who would have
created so many wonderful
picture books

Text copyright © 2002 by Mary Jane Auch
Illustrations copyright © 2002 by Herm Auch and Mary Jane Auch
All Rights Reserved
Printed and bound in July 2016 at Toppan Leefung, DongGuan City, China.
www.holidayhouse.com
11 12
Library of Congress Cataloging-in-Publication Data
Auch, Mary Jane.
The princess and the pizza / by Mary Jane Auch;
illustrated by Herm Auch and Mary Jane Auch.
p. cm.
Summary: An out-of-work princess applies to become the bride of Prince Drupert,
but first she must pass several tests, including a cooking contest.
ISBN 0-8234-1683-6 (hardcover)
ISBN 0-8234-1798-0 (paperback)
[1. Princesses—Fiction. 2. Cookery—Fiction. 3. Fairy tales.
4. Humorous stories.] I. Auch, Herm, ill. II. Title.
PZ8.A9234 Pr2002
[E]—dc21   2001024112

ISBN-13: 978-0-8234-1683-7 (hardcover)
ISBN-13: 978-0-8234-1798-8 (paperback)

Princess Paulina needed a job. Her father had given up his throne to become a wood-carver and moved them to a humble shack in a neighboring kingdom. Since the king was still learning, his carvings didn't sell, and Paulina's garden barely kept enough on the table.

Paulina missed princessing. She missed walking the peacock in the royal garden, surveying the kingdom from the castle tower, and doing the princess wave in royal processions.

Paulina tried walking a stray chicken around her shack, but it only pecked at her bare toes. Surveying the kingdom from the shack's leaky roof made even more holes. She tried princess-waving to the townspeople from her father's cart, but nobody bothered to wave back. They just thought she was swatting at flies.

One day, a page rode past the shack, announcing that Queen Zelda of Blom was seeking a true princess to become the bride of her son, Prince Drupert.

"This is my chance to get back to princessing," Paulina cried. She rummaged through her trunk of ex-princess stuff, brushed the wood shavings from her best ball gown, and blew away the bits of sawdust that clung to her diamond tiara. Then she tucked a piece of garlic into her bodice for good luck, snipped some fragrant herbs to cover up the garlic smell, and headed for the castle.

Paulina didn't expect much competition. There wasn't another princess for hundreds of miles. But when she got to Blom Castle, Paulina found she was only one of twelve princesses hoping to become the royal bride.

When she looked into her assigned room, Paulina saw her bed piled with sixteen mattresses. "Oh, for Pete's sake. The old princess-and-the-pea trick. That's so once-upon-a-time." Naturally, Paulina didn't sleep all night because she felt the lumpy pea through all of the mattresses.

When the twelve princesses gathered in the throne room the next morning, the seven who looked bright-eyed were sent home. Now only Paulina and four other sleepy princesses remained.

First, they were made to write essays entitled "Why I Want to Have the Gracious and Exquisitely Beautiful Queen Zelda for My Mother-in-Law."

Prince Drupert and Queen Zelda finally appeared on the balcony.
Queen Zelda did all the talking. "Congratulations, ladies, you have
written some lovely essays, which I will keep in my scrapbook. And
you have all passed the mattress test. But to make absolutely
sure you are of royal blood, there is a second test. Only a true
princess can wear these glass slippers."

"For Pete's sake, you never heard of sneakers?" Paulina asked.

Queen Zelda gave Paulina a sharp look. "Nobody said you had
to hike in them. Just try them on."

After the royal page made his way around the room with the slippers, two big-footed princesses were sent home. Now only Paulina and two others remained. One was followed around by seven strange little men, and the other had such a long braid dragging behind her, Paulina kept tripping over it.

"For Pete's sake, you never heard of scissors?" Paulina cried.

Queen Zelda glared at Paulina.

"You all have passed the second princess test. Your final task is to cook a feast that proves you worthy of being my dear Drupert's wife."

This set up a wail among the princesses, especially Paulina. "For Pete's sake. You have no royal chef?"

"Silence!" said the queen. "The table holds the makings for three fine feasts. Choose well, for the winner will become my dear Drupert's bride."

As Paulina started for the table, the long-haired princess tripped her, then loaded up with food. By the time Paulina got there, the seven strange little men had run off with everything but some flour, yeast, water, three overripe tomatoes, and a hunk of stale cheese.

"Hey, that's not fair! Queen Zelda, will you help me?"

"No," said the queen. "Because you have a big mouth."

A servant escorted Paulina to her room and locked the door. "Hey! How can I cook without a bowl or spoons or pots?"

There was no reply.

Paulina tried to make bread, kneading the flour, water, and yeast together; but it only stuck to the tray in a flattened mess. She squished the tomatoes over the dough to brighten it up. It looked awful. She sprinkled cheese gratings over the top. It was still a mess, and Paulina was exhausted.

"For Pete's sake, where's your fairy godmother when you need her? I'm going to take a nap." She reached under the pile of mattresses, pulled out the offending pea, and climbed into bed.

She hadn't been sleeping long when there was a knock at the door.

"Only twenty minutes left," called Queen Zelda. "I don't smell anything cooking."

"I'm not cooking," said Paulina. "I'm napping. Then I'm going home."

"You're not going anywhere," said the queen. "The losers will be beheaded."

Paulina sat bolt upright. "Beheaded! You didn't tell us that!"

"I forgot," said the queen.

"Can't I have a second chance? How about I try to spin straw into gold? Or maybe I could guess a weird little man's name?"

"No second chances," declared the queen.

"But that's not fair!" Paulina cried.

"Who needs to be fair? I'm the queen."

Paulina leaped out of bed and ran
to the window, but it was an unbelievably
long drop to the ground. The meal was
her only hope. She rushed the tray over
to the fireplace, stirred the few
remaining hot coals, then crushed
her garlic and sprinkled it over the
mess for good luck. Finally, Paulina
tossed on the herbs to cover up
the garlic smell.

Paulina paced back and forth, planning her escape. Perhaps she could make a deal with the long-haired princess to climb down her braid. She didn't notice that the goopy dough had browned into a crust, the tomatoes were bubbling, the hard bits of cheese had melted, and the fragrance of garlic and herbs filled the room.

A page opened the door. "Time's up."

Paulina took a deep breath and carried her tray into the great dining room.

The other princesses had made lovely feasts, especially the one who had the seven strange little men to help her.

Prince Drupert went right to Paulina's tray. "It's not pretty, but it smells scrumptious." He helped himself to an unusually generous piece. "What do you call this dish?"

Paulina shrugged. "I don't know."

"It can't be an official entry in the contest if it doesn't have a name," said the queen.

"Oh, for Pete's sake," Paulina muttered.

"What's that?" snapped the queen. "Pete's what?"

Remembering the beheading threat, Paulina frantically tried to think of a name. "It's Pete's . . . ah . . ."

"Pizza?" The queen took a big bite. "Odd name, but it's tasty. The winner is Paulina's pizza."

"You mean I won't be beheaded?"

"I was only kidding about the beheading," said the queen.

"Then I was only kidding about wanting to marry Prince Drupert. Who needs him? I have other plans."

"Will you leave your recipe?" asked the queen.

"No way," said Paulina. "It's just become a family secret." She headed for the door.

"I liked you best," whined the queen, following close behind.

"Oh, for Pete's sake," muttered Paulina as she stomped across the drawbridge.

TODAY'S SPECIALS

Butterscotch-Broccoli   Pickle-Parsnip
Chocolate-Chicken   Rosemary-Rhubarb
          Avocado-Apricot

Princess Paulina's Pizza Palace opened a few weeks later. It featured unusual, carved furniture and fifty kinds of pizza.

Every Thursday, on the royal chef's night off, Queen Zelda and Prince Drupert came to Paulina's for popcorn-pineapple pizza. They often stayed to play cards with Paulina's father.

From then on, whenever Paulina drove her pizza delivery cart through town doing the princess wave, everybody waved back and ran after her, asking about the day's specials.

Life was good. Paulina was grateful not to have Queen Zelda for a mother-in-law, but she still worried about one little thing.

She worried about getting Queen Zelda
as her stepmother!